I072524 3

My Kink Adventure

By Aimee Nicole

For Mel, my person.
Thank you for helping to keep me on the most
authentic path.
We all know what happens when I try to go it alone.

A Choose Your Own Adventure...

First, you will need to decide how to address your dominant. What fits you best?

If you choose a Mistress adventure—*turn to page 7*. If you choose a Sir adventure—*turn to page 8*.
If you choose a Master adventure—*turn to page 9*. If you choose a Daddy adventure—*turn to page 10*.

Unfortunately the author of this book is a brat and has decided that everyone should have a Daddy.

Please return to page 6 and select the correct answer.

Unfortunately the author of this book is a brat and has decided that everyone should have a Daddy. Please return to page 6 and select the correct answer.

Unfortunately the author of this book is a brat and has decided that everyone should have a Daddy.

Please return to page 6 and select the correct answer.

While doing some research for your contract, you decide to look into hard limits. There are so many kinky acts you didn't even know existed!

You know that you can always add hard limits later as needed…or even remove hard limits as you become more flexible over time. A true dominant gives you what you need, not what they need.

To add anal play, spanking, and fisting as hard limits to your contact, *turn to page 11*.

To add scat, needles, blood, and animal play as hard limits to your contact, *turn to page 12*.

To add play with (and in front of) any other partners as a hard limit to your contact, *turn to page 13*.

If you decide not to set any hard limits right now, *turn to page 14*.

You aren't into feeling like a child who is put in time out. Also, back door play…no thanks.

Daddy revises the contract per your request. *Turn to page 15.*

No shade to others but that stuff is just not gonna happen. Not now and not ever.

Daddy revises the contract for you.
Turn to page 15.

*I kinda wanna throw my phone across the room
'cause all I see are girls too good to be true*

Jealousy doesn't look good on anyone, and especially not on you.

Daddy revises the contact for you. *Turn
to page 15.*

If anything makes you uncomfortable, you ask Daddy to add a clause allowing for revision at a later date. You want to be free to explore without restriction.

Daddy adds the language in for you.
Turn to page 15.

Daddy presents you with the contact over a very fancy home cooked meal of spaghetti and Texas Toast. Everything looks in order so you sign, blotting olive oil on the paper.

He makes a copy for you to take home and tells you to call if you have any questions.

Turn to page 16.

It's time to pick your safeword. There's the classic green, yellow, red system that is widely recognized and used.

Green for when things are good, keep going.

Yellow…switch toys, you need water or some juice, it's time to switch up positions…

Red is a complete stop to all play and release from any bondage and/or equipment.

Turn to page 17.

If you don't like that system you can always walk your own path and select a word unique to you and your partner. It's a secret handshake you and Daddy can use in public if it's time to leave or if you need help. You should choose a word that would never be used during play.

If you decide to stick with the green, yellow, red system (it's a classic for a reason), *turn to page 18.*

If you decide to use the safeword tater tot turn to *page 19.*

If you decide to use the safeword Hufflepuff turn to *page 19.*

If you decide to use the safeword Willy Wonka turn *to page 19.*

If it ain't broke don't fix it, right?

This system seems easiest to use, I mean you see streetlights all the time...

Turn to page 20.

Having a unique safeword is really fun. It takes you back to those secret handshakes you used to do with your friends in the hall between class.

You like that you can use the word without drawing too much attention in public as well. If you called out red in front of others, they would know something was wrong.

Turn to page 20.

It's the night of your first session. You've been preparing all day. You did a really fancy face scrub that you usually save for special occasions.

You polished your nails purple and cut them very short, as written in the contract.

Took your time shaving and washing your body. A ritual no one else is present to witness but felt like a devoted act of service.

Turn to page 22.

Upon arrival, Daddy tells you to leave your things on the couch and walk into the bedroom…use the restroom on the way if needed.

You stop by the restroom and splash cool water onto your face, then take a look in the mirror at who you've become. You like this new person.

You walk into the bedroom and begin.
Turn to page 23.

You feel nervous choosing the outfit for your first session and settle on a simple matching red lace thong and bra set.

You layer it under a black pleather skirt and floral mesh top. The lingerie peeks through and makes you feel wild.

Turn to page 21.

Daddy tells you to repeat your safeword before you begin. You do. He tells you that you shouldn't need it, but it's important to always know what it is.

You smile. For the first time you feel in control of your body. He takes off your clothes, then takes off his own.

Today, he gives you a choice of toys since it's your first session.

If you decide you want to be blindfolded, *turn to page 24*. It's time to prove to Daddy that you trust him.

Or, if the wax seems more interesting, *turn to page 26*. You've always wanted to try it.

Daddy puts the blindfold on you, it's purple and matches your nails. You close your eyes, let the weight of it ferry you into calm.

You can feel his weight shifting on the bed, his hands trailing down your body. He licks your clit slow at first, then devours you.

You try to move your fingers through his hair, so soft…but he pins your hands down to the bed. Those strong hands gripping wrists into their cages.

You don't know how long this goes on. 10 minutes. 30? You don't ask permission. You just allow yourself to release into his mouth.

Turn to page 25.

He wipes his face on a Kleenex. It looks like his head was dunked into the pool.

Your head is swimming. Heaven. Clouds. Air. No name for it, really.

Daddy climbs up beside you and pulls your head onto his chest. He kisses your forehead and lets you bask in this wonderful feeling.

Turn to page 28.

Daddy gets a paraffin candle and a lighter. He orders you onto your stomach.

You quickly oblige. As the candle heats up you can smell it's newly licking flame. Nerves trundle around in your belly.

You are so far out of your comfort zone doing this. The first drop drips.

Turn to page 27.

The wax sears, it's blinding hot. But only for a second…then it begins to cool. The pain is intense and then relief.

He pours it onto your back this time, to see how you handle the sensation where the skin is thicker.

Yes, you crave those little drops. He moves them up, pours over your shoulder. You breathe slow, steady.

When he gets up and a wet towel to clean you, you pout disappointed…cannot believe it is already over.

Turn to page 28.

Since last night was your first session, it's time to have a clothes-on conversation with Daddy to talk about it. What's the best way to chat?

If you prefer to talk over a meal, *turn to page 29.*

If you would rather grab some tea/coffee at your favorite local shop, *turn to page 30.*

If you promise to keep your clothes on…but would still rather have the talk in bed…*turn to page 31.*

You'd rather do it over text. You're worried you won't be able to say everything face-to-face this first time. Maybe next time you can do it in person.

Turn to page 32.

You both sit down at your a local breakfast spot. He's never had Johnny Cakes before so you order a side to share. It's nice sharing parts of yourself with him.

You have a hickey the size of a planet on your chest. You feel wild, wonder if anyone can detective out the wickedness barely concealed by this sheer fabric.

Turn to page 33.

Sin is packed with people this Sunday morning and there is a couple by the window having a cupcake tasting for their wedding. You decide to get a pastry to share, how can you resist?

You linger a few extra moments at the barista bar, adding oat milk to your tea, stirring it around and around. Just a few extra seconds to watch him sitting there by the hanging prints, a sex Daddy out among all us regular folks.

Turn to page 33.

How quickly this became the safe haven. The place
that nurtured you with healing. You don't want to
leave, not even for breakfast. It's true you have to
wear clothes, but no one said you had to wear panties.

You sit and wait for him to finish brushing his teeth,
your long baseball jersey barely covering ass. Ok,
clothes on conversation. You can do this. Clothes
mostly on.

Turn to page 33.

It's just easier this way, now. If you are going to get it all out, you need to be able to say every word without someone interrupting your thoughts. Once you are interrupted, you lose your thought process. The rest is a garbled, incoherent mess.

One day, you hope to graduate to she who speaks wisely and effectively. *Fingers Crossed*

Turn to page 33.

The conversation is going well, you like that Daddy is willing to listen to all of your feedback and seems concerned with your satisfaction. You decide your contract is good as written. For now, it doesn't need any major changes. The one request you have is:

A little more time spent on aftercare. If you want extra cuddles, *turn to page 34.*

You want all play to be negotiated beforehand. If you like having a play-by-play structured out, *turn to page 35.*

You want a text message good morning and good night. If you like constant communication, *turn to page 36.*

No changes for now, but you can always have another clothes-on conversation later to discuss.

Turn to page 37.

"If you want I can even bring you a snack and some water," Daddy says.

You beam.

"Even those princess gummy bears?"

"Of course," he says and kisses the top of your head.

Could it always have been this good? Why did you wait so long!

Turn to page 37.

"I get it, you like a man with a plan," Daddy teases. You giggle.

"I know, it seems silly. I don't like surprises."

"That's not silly at all," he says. "Sex itineraries coming right up."

You exhale all the tension you'd been holding for who knows how long. Years.

Finally, you could negotiate your way into getting what you truly needed.

Turn to page 37.

"Done and done," Daddy confirms.

You smile knowing you won't ever have to fall asleep alone again. Someone will be there to begin and end each day with you.

"We make a pretty good team," you say.

He kisses the top of your forehead and you know you've never said anything more true in your life.

Turn to page 37.

Daddy has decided to buy you a gift of your choosing.

You've been having a hard time sleeping at night and he knows a present will make you smile. You are already beaming and don't know what to pick! He counts to three and you blurt out the first thing that comes to your mind.

If you choose a stuffy, *turn to page 38*.

If you choose a home cooked treat, courtesy of Daddy, *turn to page 39*.

If you choose Godiva chocolates, *turn to page 40*.

If you decide you want your choice of toys for the night, *turn to page 41*.

Daddy takes you to the stuffie store and you are surrounded by stuffies that need a new home. There are so many to choose from: puppies, kittens, penguins, giraffes, and those scary dolls you definitely will not take home. You decide on a huge teddy bear that you can barely carry out of there.
Hey, he said it was your choice!

Turn to page 42.

Daddy tells you to wait in bed while he prepares your surprise. You watch some Schitt's Creek and end up falling asleep. The smell of gooey chocolate wakes you. You wander into the kitchen and find him cooling chocolate chip cookies on a rack. He scolds you for not following directions and shoos you back into bed.

You sigh but do as told. He comes in a few minutes later with chocolate chip cookies topped with vanilla ice cream, melting into a warm puddly mess. He spoons it into your mouth and it's the best tasting treat you've ever had.

Turn to page 42.

The next day after work, Daddy brings you two bags of the Godiva dark chocolate ganache hearts. You eat them together while watching your favorite show, *Schitt's Creek*. He trails his fingers loosely through your hair and puts you to sleep.

Turn to page 42.

You know exactly what to pick. You choose the sex tape…looks exactly like heavy duty duck tape but neon pink.

Daddy wraps it around your head, covering your mouth. He asks your to flash your safe signal and you hold up two fingers.

"Good girl," he says. Then he grabs you by the hair and turns you over to take you from behind. You moan into the tape and when he cums inside you, the moans turn into a scream.

He flips you over and eats your pussy, cum leaking out of you.

Turn to page 42.

You have a migraine (again). The weather in New England is so up and down—last night it was 12 degrees and today it's 55.

sigh

You heard a rumor that sex can help ease physical pain.

Do you ask Daddy to give you orgasms to try and help ease the pain (*turn to page 43*) or let him pamper you with chocolates and a silent movie (*turn to page 45*).

You tell him you aren't feeling well and ask him to make it better. He asks what he can do.

"Sex please, Daddy."

You ask him to go get your vibrator and ask please for some sensory deprivation. No big noise, you tell him.

He smiles and touches your cheek. Of course, he will. He tells you to lie back and get comfortable.

Turn to page 44.

Daddy puts ear plugs in your ears, and the purple facemask over your eyes. Already you are glad to be in a quieter world.

He eats your pussy, makes you so wet before he enters you.

Distraction, pleasure, relinquishment of control. You aren't sure what eases your pain. All that matters is that it works.

You press hips up into the vibrator and relief surges through you.

Turn to page 46.

You know you can always count on Daddy to have chocolate around. Okay…maybe it's not necessarily for you because he sort of eats like a child. But you get to reap the benefits often so it's a definite win.

He brings you some double chocolate brownies and turns on Modern Times. You've seen it before, but not since college.

He tucks the blankets up to your shoulders and kisses your forehead before climbing into bed behind you. His body feels like a heated blanket, and you fall asleep before your favorite scene in the cafe.

Turn to page 46.

Things are going well, and you feel very stable in your d/s dynamic. Since open communication has built up trust, you are willing to explore things that were once outside of your comfort zone. You and Daddy decide to create a Tinder profile to search for a unicorn that will join in on a threesome.

Do you decide to post a profile seeking for a man (*turn to page 47*) a woman (*turn to page 48*) or keep the profile open to anyone and everyone (*turn to page 53*).

You post a profile seeking a man and get so many messages. Immediately. You ask Daddy to go through them. They are mostly disrespectful and he wonders how you put up with dating this whole time.

You tell him you know your tits are great but you don't need men sending crude pictures of their balls and telling you all the nasty things they want to do to you without an invitation.

You can write better smut with a stick on the beach. Take a girl out to eat first!

He deactivates the profile after just a week and you decide to change settings to women only just to see if it's any better.

Turn to page 48.

While searching for your woman unicorn, you chat on Kik with a girl who invites her boyfriend into the messaging. He seems to brush her off and is dismissive of the boundaries you and Daddy clearly communicated. You like the girl…she's funny, gorgeous, and easy to talk to.

Do you ask the girl if she just wants to be friends? *Turn to page 49.*

Do you ask if she is willing to meet without the obnoxious boo? *Turn to page 50.*

You decide to wait it out and see if he gets less extra…or ghosts. *Turn to page 51.*

You ghost the group chat, you don't know these people and never will. *Turn to page 52.*

You ask Daddy if you can just be friends with the girl. He's ok with it. When she messages with you one on one, she won't stop flirting.

It's crossing a boundary so you unfortunately have to stop all communication.

Turn to page 52.

You reach out to her to see if she's into just meeting with the two of you…without her boo. She says she's fine with it. You talk for a few more days but then the guy starts messaging again.

She encourages him in the chat! Doesn't seem like it's going to work out. Better to just cut your losses now.

Turn to page 52.

You try turning the chat away from sex a few times, just to calm him down. You don't like the derogatory way he speaks about her (and in front of her too!).

He doesn't take direction well. He keeps sending messages like: *I can't wait to put my face in your titties* and *I'm gonna put my dick in your ass* after you said no to anal.

Daddy pulls the plug and says enough is enough. You both block them.

Turn to page 52.

It's time-consuming chatting with people, but finding the right fit is really important! It sort of feels like dating again.

You don't want to end up in a dangerous situation. Anyone disrespectful of your d/s dynamic is not a good match.

Even if it's just for an hour of fun, consent and clear communication is paramount. Better to know upfront that the vibe is off.

Turn to page 54.

You like seeing all the profiles, it's a good mix of people. Unfortunately, it's mostly men who respond and they are not pleasant to chat with. They mostly just tell Daddy how "hot" you are and that they want to fuck you. Not very respectful of a d/s relationship.

He gets a little tired of it and decides to change to filter to allow women only.

Turn to page 48.

It's Christmas. You want to get your Daddy a sexy gift but know gifts will be exchanged in front of his parents.

Do you get him a second vanilla gift that won't raise any eyebrows? *Turn to page 55.*

Do you give him nothing in front of his parents… one gift is plenty! *Turn to page 56.*

You buy him a copy of the latest bestseller from his favorite author. It has to be special ordered because it comes out just two days before Christmas.

He is so thrilled to receive it, you have to hide it so he will play with you instead of immersing himself in the mystery.

Turn to page 57.

His parents seem unsure of your relationship since no gifts were exchanged. But you brought some homemade sugar cookies and gave him a card ordered from Pretty Inappropriate on Etsy when gifts were opened. Thankfully he didn't show it around.

Turn to page 57.

Finally you are alone and you can give him his real gift. The first paddle you purchased was cheap and just a starter. This one made by Glutton for Punishment will make him feel like a real Daddy boss when he uses it on your cute juicy ass. The design is based on Rocky Horror Picture Show.

You pull up your skirt so he can test it. All through dinner you wiggle in your seat, the bruise developing slow like film.

Turn to page 58.

You want to learn to deep throat for Daddy. It seems like something that's only done in porn, but you think you can hack it.

Do you ask your friends if they have any tips? *Turn to page 59.*

Do you scour kink forums for advice? *Turn to page 60.*

Do you decide to decide to stick with good old internet research so no one knows what you are up to in case it goes south? *Turn to page 62.*

Do you order some romance books from the library to see how those girls do it? *Turn to page 61.*

You ask your girlfriends at book club (an excuse to drink beer and margs at Laura's Bar and Grill) the following weekend.

They are all useless. No one deep throats…and most of them only give oral when it's earned.

This is something you don't quite understand. Pleasure that is earned and not pleasure for pleasure's sake.

Alas, you must go back to the beginning and try a new tactic (*back to page 58*).

Ok…some pretty helpful advice from these more advanced kinksters.

1. Don't use any numbing lube.
2. Don't eat beforehand.
3. Find a position that works for you.
4. Don't forget to breathe.
5. Use lots of spit.
6. Have Daddy rub your throat with affection while deep throating and coax you with words of affection.

Turn to page 63.

You order five of the highest rated romance books from the local library.

When they come in, you sit down with some hot tea and those mini chocolate chip cookies from Trader Joe's that are impossible to eat just one of.

Unfortunately, all of these protagonists are perfect at everything "sex" and you just can't relate.

They never gag when giving head/deep throating. They always cum on demand/at the same time as their partner/500 times a night. They are always just tragic enough to be totally irresistible but not damaged.

You return the books and vow to write realistic romance characters if you ever decide to walk that path.

Not a successful venture. But that's ok, you can always try again!

Turn back to page 58.

You fire up Duck Duck Go (don't need the man tracking your searches for this one) and find a blog post written by a gay man that seems very promising.

You decide to start with the advice immediately. Three times a day you brush the back of your tongue with your toothbrush. You gag profusely.

After about a week, it's not quite so bad. You are ready to try out your new not-so-bratty throat on Daddy.

Turn to page 63.

Feeling somewhat prepared, you decide to test out your surprise for Daddy.

You ask him to lay back and he, thankfully, obliges.

You lean over him, between his legs. Grab his dick with your left hand and tease it for a minute or two. Slowly you work it back.

Immediately, you gag towards the back of your throat. But you aren't deterred. You keep going, knowing you have to continue to relax the muscles.

It's not exactly a sexy success today, but over time it will be. You're sure of it!

Turn to page 64.

You read about Shibari in the Fetlife chats. The photos are beautiful and you want to be wrapped up in rope like those girls too. Daddy doesn't see too thrilled about the prospect of investing his time in this skill. You are disappointed.

You tell him to learn Shibari or get himself another sub…arms crossed and hip protruding at the risk of a spanking. *Turn to page 65.*

You decide to wait a few months before asking again. There are plenty of other things to do while he warms up to the idea. *Turn to page 66.*

Daddy raises an eyebrow and dismisses you for the day. You pout and say you aren't going anywhere. He tells you to pick a punishment that fits your subordination.

You get ice cream from the freezer and two spoons. He laughs and shakes his head. Not exactly what he had in mind?

You must have caught him in a good mood. You eat ice cream together and talk about other things you found on Fet, but the Shibari conversation is dropped for now.

Turn to page 67.

Maybe he will warm up to the idea if he feels like it was *his* idea down the road. You decide to find some really good porn with Shibari later on. A nice easing into it.

He's still the Daddy, and you respect that. He does needs time to learn after all.

Turn to page 67.

Daddy orders you onto your stomach, but you are feeling bratty so you push him away and leave red scratches all down his chest. He chuckles and flips you over. You grumble and make a silent vow to hide his weights in a closet when he's not looking.

He manages to handcuff you to the bed despite your half-hearted squirms. You can't see what he's up to but hear the top of a lube bottle flick open. Cool liquid slides down your ass and you automatically arch up for him.

Turn to page 68.

Daddy asks if you are ready and you moan "Yes, Daddy." The butt plug glides in easily…a little too easily. You him him say "Uh oh," and ask what happened.

He says, "I can't see it anymore."

Do you stay calm and trust him to get it out (*turn to page 69*) or do you freak the fuck out (*turn to page 70*).

You trust that your Daddy will take care of you. He plunges his fingers inside and is able to remove the plug after a minute or two.

He unties you from the bed and you both laugh about how funny it was, you almost got on that Netflix show making fun of people who end up in the ER for goofy medical mishaps!

Turn to page 72.

You immediately start thrashing because something is stuck up your butt! You can feel it lodged inside and don't know what to do.

Daddy asks if you want to go to the hospital and you say yes. They remove it easily, but now you have to have a clothes-on discussion about trust and limits.

Turn to page 71.

After the "ordeal," Daddy gets you home safely. All you want is a shower and pajamas.

After some self-care, Daddy asks what happened earlier. You tell him you are sorry, that you were scared. He says he understands and that he's sorry it happened. He asks you to trust him to take care of you.

You say it's something you are working on, it takes a long time for you to build up trust. You suggest weekly date nights for clothes on conversation only.

He smiles and says it's a great idea. Friday night date nights. First up, build your own burgers.

Turn to page 72.

It's your first Valentine's Day together. Daddy is taking you to a scratch Mexican kitchen you both like.

You put on a lacy red thong, short leather skirt, and mesh top—hoping to turn more heads than just his.

It's a special day and you want to do something small for him. After a lot of back and forth you, think you have just the thing.

A handmade Etsy card with nude Polaroids enclosed (*turn to page 73*).

A dirty story you hope he will act out after reading (*turn to page 74*).

Homemade heart shaped chocolates (*turn to page 75*).

New nipple clamps with charms that say "Property of Daddy" (*turn to page 76*).

You order the card so it arrives early and get to work taking the pictures. You have to focus mostly on titty shots because you don't know how to use the timer. You take some with lingerie…and some without. They look fantastic!

Turn to page 77.

You have a lot of fun writing the story. You really want him to use the new high heat wax candles you bought months ago, so you work that in.

He doesn't rely heavily on toys to dominate you, but sometimes you like the toys! You hope he will like the story and can't wait for him to read it after dinner.

Turn to page 77.

You scour Pinterest for recipes, reading reviews and making sure you pick a good one. You don't want to have to make it twice! You choose white and milk chocolate so there is a good mix. You get the molds at a craft store (weird?) and they come out perfect.

You even taste test a couple of each to make sure they come out ok. Hey, it's part of the process, right?

Turn to page 77.

You find a shop on Etsy that makes custom nipple clamps. They will laser your chosen words onto the charm. You have to put a rush order in because you took so long to decide on the right ones, but it's worth it.

When the box comes in, it's wrapped with a beautiful bow so you decide not to open it before giving him the gift. Hopefully everything is spelled right!

Turn to page 77.

The dinner is so delicious. You order your favorite meal: veggie enchiladas. He gets some dish piled high with meat.

You slide your gift across the table, heart beating so fast you think it might fly away.

He smiles so wide and reaches for your hand. "Thank you baby," he says. "I'm so lucky to have you."

You made the right choice.

Turn to page 78.

Daddy surprises you with a new paddle. The plastic has sharp pointy teeth. You tilt hips up in anticipation.

Daddy hits his own hand a few times to test the weight of it, then strikes.

You yelp. Unsure of the feeling.

Do you safeword (*turn to page 79*) or let him try it again to see if you like it (*turn to page 80*).

You call out your safeword. He puts the paddle down and lies next to you, his face so close to yours.

"Are you ok?" he asks.

"I didn't like it. Maybe we can try again another day, but not today."

"That's ok, baby," he says.

He proceeds to lick your pussy while you wrap your legs around his neck. Any memory of the evil paddle is wiped away.

Turn to page 81.

You aren't too sure about his new friend, but you don't want to make any snap judgments.

He caresses the skin where he paddles between each hit. It feels magical. Pain mixed with pleasure.

Ok, maybe you can get used to this…

Turn to page 81.

Daddy has assigned you homework for this week's upcoming session. He wants you to create a playlist and you are getting mixtape flashbacks from high school.

There are so many sex songs to choose from, you don't even know where to begin. You decide the pace is ultimately going to be the structural and most foundational factor.

Do you want to keep it slow and sensual (*turn to page 82*) or upbeat and fast (*turn to page 83*).

Maybe if you keep it slow and sensual, the session will last for hours! You love a good tease *wink.*

There are so many good songs and by the time you finish searching, it's dark outside.

Here are some songs you come up with:

—Waiting Game by Banks

—Pleasure This Pain by Kwamie Liv

—Nothing's Gonna Hurt You Baby by Cigarettes After Sex

—Two Weeks by FKA Twigs

—Mirror Massa (I Think I'm Falling for Ya) by Dathan

Turn to page 84.

Maybe if you have a fast-paced playlist, he will be inspired to select the naughtiest toys! Here's what you decide on (to start):

—Body Talk by 1st Vows

—Lovers by Anna of the North

—Go to Town by Doja Cat

—Don't Blame Me by Taylor Swift

—Hells Round the Corner by Tricky

Turn to page 84.

You pour yourself a drink, that was a lot of work. You're feeling inspired by all the creative lyrics.
Thankfully the playlist can be modified any time. Add more songs later on when you think of them so you won't forget!

1.______________________________________

2.______________________________________

3.______________________________________

4.______________________________________

5.______________________________________

Turn to page 85.

You're pretty proud of the playlist you've created so far. Now it's time to name the playlist so you can find it easily. You decide not to stress too much over it, you can always change the name if you think of something later that's a better fit.

Turn to page 86 if you name your playlist <u>Weekday Workout</u> (You don't want anyone to know you have a sex playlist!)

Turn to page 87 if you name your playlist <u>Working Girl</u> (I mean, you are!)

Turn to page 88 if you name your playlist <u>Daddy's Mixtape</u>.

Okay so maybe you aren't queen of cardio or anything, which will make it even easier to spot this playlist as it has no competition. Sex is cardio…it's like a naked pilates.

Turn to page 89.

Shoutout to all the working girls everywhere. You wish you'd grown up in a world where girls could aspire to be anything they could dream into being.

Life certainly was no princess fairytale.

It does feel like you are breaking the mold just a little bit. Raising two middle fingers up to conventional sexual politics.

Turn to page 89.

Can't get anymore classic than that. Plus, it's a love letter, to Daddy.

Turn to page 89.

Daddy has to go away on a business trip…for a week. You are very unhappy about it but are trying hard to stifle the brat.

He tells you not to worry, he will make sure to keep connected while he's apart.

Do you ask for a new stuffie to cuddle while he's gone? *Turn to page 90.*

Do you request daily zoom calls over dinner to catch up about the day? *Turn to page 94.*

Do you negotiate a minimum number of texts to be exchanged throughout the day to ensure you don't get lonely? *Turn to page 95.*

…Or do you want it all? Brats do have very high attention needs after all. *Turn to page 90.*

He says you can have a new stuffie, but jokes that soon there won't be enough room for him on the bed if you keep collecting them.

Do you burst out into tears…so sensitive at the prospect of him leaving for so long! *Turn to page 91.*

Or do you grab 5 stuffies and move them to the couch. They will be happy there anyway, prime movie night position! *Turn to page 92.*

You can't help it; you crumble to the floor in a meltdown. You haven't been apart this long from each other since your d/s relationship began.

It feels like he's stuffing half of you in his suitcase and taking it with him. To boring business meetings!

He tells you to make plans with friends at least two nights. You agree, reluctantly.

Turn to page 93.

You hastily grab all the puppy stuffies and bring them to the couch with a huff. Some dogs really do enjoy tv. You will put on animal planet for them later.

Turn to page 93.

At the stuffie store you choose a blue unicorn stuffie.
You name her Marilyn. You know she will be good
for this trip because she is extra stuffed and pleasant
to hug.

Turn to page 96.

If a brat requiring all the attention, *turn to page 94.*

To make the zoom calls work you will have to eat around 8PM due to the time difference. Maybe you will try to make some more complicated recipes than pasta or eggs with that extra time.

You will definitely be eating in bed. Nothing he can say about that, he won't even be here to stop you!

Turn to page 96.

If a brat requiring all the attention, *turn to page 95.*

"How many texts would you like to receive from me each day?" he asks.

"50."

Daddy laughs. "I'll be in a lot of meetings, it's a work trip not a vacation baby."

"Please Daddy." You pout your lip real good and bury your head in his shoulder.

"How can I refuse you?" He sighs.

You smile wider than a cat o nine tail's strike.

Turn to page 96.

You ask Daddy what his fantasy is. He's been so busy pleasing and pleasuring you that you never thought to ask what would drive him wild.

He says he wants you to wear a butt plug with a long silky fox tail. *Turn to page 97.*

He wants more public sex…and he wants to be caught. *Turn to page 102.*

You can definitely make that happen! You hop on Etsy when you get home and find lots of real fur tails which sort of freak you out. You decide to go for the faux fur option.

Turn to page 98.

They have tails with the plug attached…or you can select a detachable option. That seems best because it will be easier to clean and you can also switch out the size.

Hmm…what size do you decide to get?

Small—obviously. You are still warming up to having things (anything) in there. *Turn to page 99.*

Medium. You think you can handle it. *Turn to page 100.*

Large. Time to make him wild. *Turn to page 101.*

You present your new toy the next time you see Daddy. He takes it from you and orders you to strip naked, lie face down.

You know he likes it already.

He gets the lube and gets your ass nice and wet. To your surprise, the plug doesn't hurt going in.

Daddy enters your pussy from behind and tugs at your tail. You moan into the pillow and have discovered a new fetish.

Turn to page 105.

You present your new toy the next time you see Daddy. He takes it from you and orders you to strip naked, lie face down.

You know he likes it already.

He gets the lube and gets your ass nice and wet. Daddy is gentle, he works in the plug nice and slow. When it pops all the way in you feel it's weight within you, filling you with pleasure.

Daddy enters your pussy from behind and tugs at your tail. You moan into the pillow and have discovered a new fetish.

Turn to page 105.

You present your new toy the next time you see Daddy. He takes it from you and orders you to strip naked, lie face down.

You know he likes it already.

He gets the lube and gets your ass nice and wet. He stretches you first with his fingers. You clench your fists as Daddy tries to work the plug in.

"Take a deep breath baby," he says.

You do. You relax with intention. He finally pops in the plug and you feel so much satisfaction that you were able to overcome this obstacle.

Daddy enters your pussy from behind and tugs at your tail. You moan into the pillow and have discovered a new fetish.

Turn to page 105.

You like this idea…you think.

"Where?" You ask.

"There is a hiking trail right off the state park. Let's go there tomorrow, it's supposed to be good weather."

Turn to page 103.

You wear a skirt, no panties. Always the best choice for public play, he can lift it right up and get to business

He leads you up the trail and after a quarter mile, there is a big rock to the left. You both go sneak behind it.

He bends you over the top where anyone walking down the path can see you.

Turn to page 104.

It's exciting, but you keep lookout for any kids. Those scouting troops earning their badges or something like that.

A woman comes, riding her bike but doesn't see you. An older man walks by smoking a cigarette, not noticing anything off the path.

You realize that everyone is so wrapped up in their own world, you don't need to worry so much about being caught…even in such a public place.

Turn to page 105.

Daddy's birthday is coming up soon and you want to surprise him with a sexy new outfit.

You decide to shop online because you are having trouble finding the right size in store. You order a sexy schoolgirl outfit and try it on as soon as it arrives.

Turn to page 106.

The cute white halter top breaks the second you put it on!

Titties just spill out all over. Now you don't have a top to wear as part of the outfit…

Do you rock the cute tie, skirt, and thong anyway… you can make it work! *Turn to page 107.*

Do you panic and try to rush another order in time for his special day? *Turn to page 108.*

Do you decide to scratch the sexy outfit and just surprise him in your birthday suit…that's where this is all going anyway! *Turn to page 109.*

Daddy walks into the bedroom and sees you in your (almost complete) very sexy outfit. He drops his bag and immediately grabs your ass, pulling you close.

No time to grab toys or pull off all the clothes, he bends you over the bed and plunges into you.

Guess you didn't need that stupid halter top after all…

Turn to page 110.

You bypass customer service. You want it replaced but need it by the end of the week to have it in time for his birthday.

Thankfully they offer overnight shipping for an exorbitant price. You place another order and it arrives in time for his special day.

The next top fits a bit better and you are so relieved. You look amazing!

Turn to page 110.

Now you aren't even sure why you spent money on this silly outfit in the first place. Sure dressing up can be fun and all, but isn't the goal just to end up naked?

You perch on the lip of the bed naked, waiting for Daddy.

When he sees you upon entering, he drops his bags and strips in record time. He pushes you back onto the mattress and worships your body like never before. It feels like your birthday, not his. No complaints here.

Turn to page 110.

It's been an exhausting day. You had work meetings back-to-back and your boss decided to shadow your presentation last minute.

Your lunch fell on the floor, so you ate some stale crackers pillaged from the break room.

Traffic home was unusually dense due to yet another tour of Hamilton.

Turn to page 111.

You finally get home, take a long shower, then pull on some tattered college sweats.

Your phone screen flashes "Daddy" just as you settle in with a bowl of pasta and are about to click play on the next episode of Love is Blind.

Do you answer the call (*turn to page 113*) or decide to call him back when you are in a better mood (*turn to page 112*).

You've taken care of yourself your whole life. You certainly don't need some guy stepping in this late in the game to mess up your tried-and-true self care system.

You press play on the remote and twirl capellini around your fork, careful to twist in some parmesan cheese with each bite.

Turn to page 135.

"Hello?" You grumble through the speaker.
"Come outside, baby," he says.
You click the angry red hang up button and shove your feet into slippers. So demanding! How dare he!

Turn to page 114.

You yank open the door to a steaming hot pizza and your favorite bottle of wine.

"Mondays are the worst," he says. "Let's stuff ourselves full until we can't walk."

You grab the wine and wave him in.

Do you take the food into the bedroom (*turn to page 115*) or to the living room (*turn to page 117*).

You leave your slippers at the door and grab two wine glasses from the kitchen.

"Follow me," you order.

Daddy laughs and shakes his head. Still, he does as he's told and follows you into the bedroom.

Turn to page 116.

You pour two very full glasses and lift one to your lips.

"Hold on, we're going to make it a little more interesting. Ever played never have I ever?" he asks.

Turn to page 120.

You grab two wine glasses from the kitchen and take a seat on the couch.

"I'm so glad you came, today was a shit day," you sigh.

"I'm sorry, baby. Want to talk about it?"

Obviously you want to talk about it, why else would you let him in? *Turn to page 118.*

Fuck no, let's just eat and fuck. *Turn to page 119.*

You launch into a very detailed explanation of why today was completely unacceptable and therefore needs to be cancelled from your memory... immediately.

He laughs a little too loud at the part where you scream about salad dressing being spilled all down your shirt, creating a sheer magic illusion every time you turned to the side.

I've got an idea to help you relax." He tops off your wine glass. "We're going to play Never Have I Ever —strip version"

Turn to page 120.

"I'm over it," you say. "I just want to eat more of this pizza then have you fuck my brains out until I fall asleep in a sex coma."

"Well, I can definitely arrange that…" He flips the pizza lid closed. "But first we play."

Turn to page 120.

"The stakes are a toy of choice from Mister Sister Erotica, purchased of course by the loser."

You cross your arms. "I'm not going to lose…"

"Sure baby."

Better get ahead of the game: "Never have I ever had sex in my parent's bed."

You have (*turn to page 121*).

You have never (*turn to page 122*).

"Dirty girl," Daddy teases.

You shrug and munch another slice. You won't allow any teasing to get under your skin…eye on the prize…with one less piece of clothing.

"Never have I ever had a threesome."

You have (*turn to page 123*).

You have never (*turn to page 124*).

"That's only because we did it in my parents' bed at brunch that day," he teases.

You shrug, they aren't your parents. That's not how the game works. Though the pancakes were pretty delicious…

Daddy tugs off his shirt.

"Never have I ever had a threesome."

You have (*turn to page 123*).

You have never (*turn to page 124*).

We both have to take off clothes for this," you laugh.

"Maybe I'm just trying to get you naked," Daddy winks.

You roll your eyes. Sabotage to win a game…how childish.

"Never have I ever work an anal plug in public."

You have (*turn to page 125*).

You have never (*turn to page 126*).

"Don't worry," he says. "We will check it off the bucket list one day."

You watch him take off his jeans and don't care about his experience today. Not as long as you are winning.

"Never have I ever worn an anal plug in public."

You have (*turn to page 125*).

You have never (*turn to page 126*).

"Way to throw me under the bus on that one," you sass as you wiggle out of your jeans. Damnit, you didn't want to lose.

He starts crawling towards you, but you hold out both arms. "Nice try mister! Let's finish this."

"Never have I ever masturbated more than five times in a day."

You have (*turn to page 127*).

You have never (*turn to page 128*).

"Currently adding that to my list of things to do to you," Daddy teases.

"When…"

"Doesn't your friend Emily get married soon?" Your stomach knots.

"Never have I ever masturbated more than five times in a day."

You have (*turn to page 127*).

You have never (*turn to page 128*).

Daddy raises an eyebrow.

"Well my vibrator does a really good job," you offer.

"Better than me?"

"I plead the fifth," you tease.

"You're going to get spanked for that later."

"Never have I ever been to a strip club."

You have (*turn to page 129*).

You have never (*turn to page 130*).

"I've probably maxed out at like three times," you offer.

"I haven't hit 5 either," Daddy says. "A stalemate…"

"Never have I ever been to a strip club."

You have (*turn to page 129*).

You have never (*turn to page 130*).

"When?" Daddy prompts.

"Bachelorette party…obviously."

Daddy shakes his head. "I'll take you sometime, on our own, if you want."

He takes off his socks.

"Never have I ever had a wet dream."

You have (*turn to page 131*).

You have never (*turn to page 132*).

"It's not that I don't respect women making their own choices," you say. "No one has ever offered to take me before."

Daddy checks his invisible schedule.

You shove him lightly.

He takes off his socks and it's all back to business.

"Never have I ever had a wet dream."

You have (*turn to page 131*).

You have never (*turn to page 132*).

Daddy balks. "That's a well-laid trap," he gripes.

"What! I get woken up all wet down there…I feel like it counts."

"Hey if you want to dig your own grave, I'm not going to stop you."

Oh yeah…

Turn to page 133.

Daddy balks. "That's a well-laid trap," he gripes.

"All is fair in love and war."

"And which is this?"

"Clearly war…" You kiss him on the lips, slowly.

Turn to page 134.

You slip off your panties in defeat. He better pick out
a good toy…

Turn to page 135.

He pulls down his boxers, revealing it all with a spring. You've never been more excited to win any game.

"Pull out your credit card, Daddy. I'm going to run you into the red."

He bends you over and slaps your ass.

Turn to page 135.

Daddy decides to surprise you with a nice picnic at the local park. It's a beautiful day with summer finally here.

He picks up salads from the place you like and even presents you with a double chocolate cookie for dessert.

Turn to page 136.

After eating, he tells you to pick the spot you want to have some public sex to celebrate the nice weather.

You choose a golf course. You happen to have the perfect outfit for the occasion. *Turn to page 137.*

You still haven't lived out your teenage fantasy of sex in a car…and now is your chance. *Turn to page 139.*

Some might think it's a little yucky but you have this public bathroom fetish. Maybe you can even convince him to take you into a porta potty! *Turn to page 141.*

Lucky for you, he isn't a big golfer. But he has been out on the course a few times with his friends.

You pick a cloudy day around lunchtime. Lots of cars coming in for lunch, but no one really walking around the course.

You both walk over to some trees clustered around a pond and he bends you over, spanking your ass loud enough to startle birds from their nests.

Turn to page 138.

As he pumps in and out of you, you notice houses across the pond and wonder if anyone can see. You realize people could take pictures of this act, post them online. It doesn't embarrass you but makes you even hungrier for more public displays.

He finishes taking you. Leaving your panties in the car may have been sexy but it sure wasn't practical. Cum dribbles down your legs as you both run back to the parking lot.

Turn to page 144.

Daddy picks you up after work and you head down to the beach. It's still off-season and not many cars are spotted in the parking lot.

He backs up into the back corner near a dumpster. You both climb into the backseat which he has thoughtfully cleared out.

"Take off your clothes, baby," he says. And you do.

Turn to page 140.

"Climb on top of me."

He is erect and waiting for you, slides inside like a homecoming.

You start to grind your hips against him and gasp. Something about this position, his ass in a bucket seat tilted pelvis up to meet you.

He spanks you, demands more movement. You oblige and wonder how you've been missing this all along.

Turn to page 144.

"Not in a porta potty," he says.
You shrug. "Fine. Taco Bell."
He bursts out with a laugh so loud it scares your cat.

"What...? They have single stalls and I really want a chalupa."

"You drive a hard bargain."

Turn to page 142.

Upon arriving to Taco Bell you go immediately into the restroom. He puts in the order by touchscreen and knocks five times so you know it's him.

You let him in with a grin. He grabs you by the hair from behind and pushes you toward the grimy sink. It has soap spilled everywhere and is hard to hold onto.

Turn to page 143.

He pushes inside you and you bite your bottom lip to make sure you don't make a noise.

Someone knocks but you both ignore them. You look into the mirror, back into his eyes. He stares so deep inside you, you are pretty sure explosions like this is how stars are formed.

Daddy grabs some paper towels and cleans both of you up before you open the door together and walk back onto the floor. Your lunch is waiting on the counter. No one is any the wiser.

Turn to page 144.

Daddy has been playing on his phone since you arrived.

Now you are feeling especially bratty. What is so good on that phone anyway? And why isn't his attention on you?

Do you go sit on his lap and give him butterfly kisses? *Turn to page 145.*

Do you sit and pout until he notices you? *Turn to page 147.*

You climb onto his lap and lean down to give him butterfly kisses. Daddy laughs and puts down his phone.

"I'm sorry baby," he says. "Can I help you with something?"

Turn to page 146.

"Yes Daddy," you say. "My pussy needs some servicing."

"Is that so?

You stand up and push your panties to the side.

Daddy gets the paddle and gives you three swats on your pussy lips before entering.

There is nothing on his phone that could be better than this.

Turn to page 150.

You plump out your bottom lip and cross both arms. Minutes go by one after the other.

If this lasts much longer, you're going to have to pee.

Turn to page 148.

Daddy finally looks up from his phone.

"Anything wrong, baby?" he asks. "Can I do something for you?"

You sigh and throw up your hands.
"Finally! Yes, I need some attention."

Turn to page 149.

Daddy laughs. "Some sexual attention?"

You stand up and push your panties to the side.

Daddy gets the paddle and gives you three swats on your pussy lips before entering.

There is nothing on his phone that could be better than this.

Turn to page 150.

Daddy's friend is getting married and he asks if you want to go with him…as his date.

You don't really know his friend, or any of his friends for that matter.

Do you still go? Maybe there will be a dog or something you can sit in the corner with. *Turn to page 151.*

You tell Daddy that you have to catch up on work. It's not an outright lie, you do have a big presentation next week. *Turn to page 156.*

You pull out a dress from the back of the closet you haven't worn in a few months. It's red velvet and cuts a little high, which is why you don't wear it often.

But you want to feel confident walking into that room! You paint your nails a fresh coat of bright pink paint to mach.

Turn to page 152.

The ceremony takes place in the backyard and has lots of Wiccan influence. You take pictures to send to the bride after the ceremony. Candid photos are the best, and you hope someone will do the same for you when it's your day.

The afterparty turns out to be a relaxed gathering at her new house. They decided not to do your big typical hotel conference room seating which you really appreciate.

It's just a bunch of friends casually drinking and eating pizza.

Do you try to strike up conversation with some of Daddy's friends? *Turn to page 153.*

…Or do you make friends with their new adopted dog, Max? *Turn to page 154.*

It seems like all these people have been friends for a really long time. You sit down on a couch where some people are chatting about home ownership.

sigh

Can't you all just talk about sex positions or lube preferences or something? Who cares about having enough walls to hang up photos. You just shove them all in a cigar box and call it a day.

You chime in with head nods and "oh yeah's" once in a while but realize you have nothing to contribute here. And for the first time, you're ok with that.

Turn to page 155.

Max is a really precious dachshund mix the newlyweds adopted just a couple of months ago. You sit next to him on the couch and scratch his belly while some people chat about home ownership.

sigh

Can't you all just talk about sex positions or lube preferences or something? Who cares about having enough walls to hang up photos. You just shove them all in a cigar box and call it a day.

Max licks your hand before jumping down…off to find some pizza crumbs, leaving you on your own.

Turn to page 155.

You set off to find Daddy, who is in the kitchen chatting with an old friend from high school.

"Hey baby," he says. He wraps his hand around your neck and immediately you dip into sub space. Possessed and needed.

You wrap an arm around his waist and are content to stay by his side.

Turn to page 157.

"I'd really like for you to be there," Daddy says.

You chew your bottom lip. You want to spend time with him but you don't know these people.

"It will be very casual," he promises. "Do you think you can fit it in?"

You reconsider and decide to make the wedding. He wouldn't ask if he didn't want you there. *Turn to page 151.*

You stand firm and keep up the boundary. This is a big presentation, and you don't want to be distracted. Plus, you just aren't ready to meet all of his friends at one event. Maybe he can introduce you slowly one-on-one. *Turn to page 160.*

People have been drinking for a few hours now, especially Daddy. He grabs your hand every time he walks into another room.

You turn your head to see where the dog has gone because you haven't seen him in awhile.

All of a sudden you feel a sharp spank land on your ass.

You swivel back and see Daddy bearing a very mischievous grin.

Do you ask Daddy what the hell he thinks he's doing? *Turn to page 158.*

Do you decide to fight fire with fire and kiss him right in front of all these strangers? *Turn to page 159.*

"Daddy...what the fuck was that!?"

He leans down, his beer-soaked lips dangerously close to yours.

"I'm ready to take you home, baby."

"Is that a threat, Daddy."

"It most certainly is…"

It was a fun party, but the night is over when Daddy says it's over.

Turn to page 160.

You grab Daddy by the neck and pull his beer-soaked lips down to meet yours.

His doesn't resist, grabs another handful of ass to draw you close.

"Time to go," Daddy whispers. "I agree."

And you walk out to the car hand-in-hand.

Turn to page 160.

You decide you want to show your Daddy some additional acts of service. You might be a little bratty sometimes, but this will allow you to be submissive on a regular basis as you choose.

Do you want to give a cleansing blow job after sex as a thank you? This will allow you to worship Daddy and his body for all the pleasure he gives to you. *Turn to page 161.*

Do you want to cook him a big Sunday dinner of his favorite foods each week? *Turn to page 162.*

Do you want to give him little surprises throughout the week? *Turn to page 163.*

You want to do it all! You will make time to give these acts of service to Daddy as best you can. *Turn to page 161.*

You make this expectation of yourself and for yourself. After each time Daddy pleasures you, you will give him a nice blowjob to say thank you.

The expectation is not to bring him to the point of orgasm, it's to clean him with your mouth. To lick him to the point of cleanliness.

Daddy loves your devotion. He helps you up when you are still spaced out in sub space to perform this act.

Turn to page 164.

If you are performing all acts of service turn to *page 162.*

Daddy is a big eater, so you have a lot of work ahead of you. For the first dinner you decide to prepare a big Italian supper.

You make sausage, peppers, and onions. A veggie lasagna. Rolls and butter. Salad. Meatballs and gravy. It's the works and you will have leftovers for a week. Maybe you will have to freeze some…

Daddy can't believe you cooked all this food. And to be honest, neither can you!

Turn to page 164.

If you are performing all acts of service turn to *page 163.*

You scour Pinterest for some ideas. You leave him little notes in his lunch (and hope his co-workers won't see them). The notes have little drawings of him spanking you. Hopefully he can make it out, you aren't a great artist!

On a weeknight you put on some lingerie under an oversized sweater. He gets a little surprise when he unwraps you.

You tape some nude Polaroids on the bathroom mirror—that he sees first thing upon waking.

You have a lot more ideas, and plenty of time to act on them!

Turn to page 164.

You start to think about your online privacy. Are you ready to come out into the world with your kinky self?

Daddy doesn't post anything kink related, but he isn't ashamed of this lifestyle.

Turn to page 165.

You see a hilarious meme on Instagram and consider sharing it. You have some work friends and family that follow your account.

Do you say fuck it and share the meme? I mean we've all read Fifty Shades of Grey by now, right? *Turn to page 166.*

You save the photo to your phone. Maybe you will decide to share it later…but you just aren't ready for that drama yet. *Turn to page 167.*

You don't owe anyone an explanation about your life. The meme is funny, you share it and get lots of likes.

If someone wants to ask you about the content, you feel secure and confident enough in where you are to address it.

You take comfort knowing that judgment stems from insecurity. We don't all have to agree with each other, but we certainly don't need to tear each other down.

Turn to page 168.

You can laugh at the meme anytime, and you share it with Daddy over dinner.

He laughs and asks where you found it, then decides to follow the account.

One day you will catch up to him with your kinky self. One day soon.

Turn to page 168.

You want to surprise Daddy with a very sexy night in since he was sick with the flu last week.

You're glad he is starting to feel better…must be all the chicken soup you made for him from scratch!

Turn to page 169.

You find a really good porn video on Bellesa. You prefer women-on-women porn, and you know he likes it too.

You light a couple of candles, the ones that are safe to drip onto skin.

Next to the bed, you put out a bottle of massage oil from Soothing Touch. You have sensitive skin and aren't allergic to this brand.

Daddy comes into the room and becomes very dominant, ruining your plan to spoil him!

Do you push back and get bratty. You worked really hard on this surprise! *Turn to page 170.*

Do you let him take over…he is the Daddy after all. *Turn to page 171.*

"Daddy, sit!"

Daddy growls at you and pushes you onto the bed.

"No Daddy," you squirm.

He grabs your wrists and pins you down.

Do you lose the fight? *Turn to page 171.*

…Or do you continue to resist? *Turn to page 172.*

"Be a good girl, or I'll have to punish you."

"I'm sorry Daddy. I just wanted to make you feel really nice," you say.

"I appreciate it baby."

He turns you onto your stomach and turns your head towards the screen so you can see the women touch each other. One of the women is especially beautiful…covered in tattoos up and down her arms.

Daddy rubs oil all over your back and you release yourself to him.

Turn to page 174.

You lick his face and show him you are all fun and games. The brat is here to stay.

He goes to take off his clothes and you use this as your golden opportunity—you grab the oil and put it all over your hands.

"Oops…" you say.

Daddy glares at you. "That's not cool, baby."

"I'll take my punishment later Daddy, but for now lie down and relax."

Turn to page 173.

Daddy finally lies down, and you climb on top of his butt to get a good angle of his back.

He surrenders to your massage and the tension he's been carrying all week from not getting his work done and having to fight all the sick germs start to drain out.

He takes deep breaths, calmly watches the video. Allows you to pamper him.

You'll take your punishment later on. It was worth it to see him relaxed.

Turn to page 174.

Today Daddy has advised that he will be pussy worshipping you. You aren't sure what that means, but you know he will be taking you to church.

Turn to page 175.

You do a quick search online and find some weird stuff. Is this sort of like the WebMd thing? Don't look anything up online because it's scary and you will get cancer, then die.

Daddy tells you to sit in the middle of the bed. He allows you to choose your worship. You are very excited to choose!

You want to experiment with pussy slapping. You like a little bit of pain mixed with pleasure. *Turn to page 176.*

You've always been curious about fisting. Time to take your first stab at it. *Turn to page 179.*

You want to try temperature play with the glass dildo. You've wanted to do it for a long time and now's your chance! *Turn to page 181.*

Daddy puts your nipple clamps on, then takes off all his clothes. First, he slaps your outer pussy with his dick a few times.

He spreads your labia with his fingers and hits his dick onto your clit.

Over and over and over again.
It feels amazing.

Daddy asks if you want to be pussy slapped with his bare hand (*turn to page 177*) or the cat o' nine tails (*turn to page 178*).

If he isn't too bothered with toys, maybe he will shove his dick into you faster.

Daddy slaps your pussy soft at first, then firmer. You like the sensation. But then again, you like being spanked too.

You grab his dick and shove it inside of you. Daddy wraps his hand around your throat so you know who's in charge here.

Turn to page 186.

Daddy gets the cat o' nine tails from the toy chest and sits between your legs.

He starts gently dragging it across your skin so you can get used to the weight of it. Then he brings it down with a whip.

You clench your knees to his waist. He comes down again. You ball your hands into fists. Again. It's not so bad this time.

The pain mixes with pleasure and he twists his fingers inside you to alleviate the fire.

Turn to page 186.

Daddy grabs the lube…spreads it all over his hand and your pussy.

He licks your nipples, throat, stomach.

Inserts one finger, two, three. Pumps them in and out of you. He inserts four and is able to work up to the knuckle.

Turn to page 180.

You grab onto the mattress. Your pussy feels very full and stretched. You aren't sure if you can fit all of him in.

"Take some deep breaths, baby."

You do.

Daddy tries to curl his fingers inside you. He has really big hands. Pitcher's hands.

After about a half hour of pussy worship he pulls out his hand and starts fucking you.

"We will practice this another day," he promises. "This is only the beginning.

Turn to page 186.

"Finally we can use the glass dildo," you say.

Do you want to do heat play (*turn to page 182*) or ice play (*turn to page 184*).

Daddy goes to warm up some water. You apply bright red lipstick and take sexy photos, set one as the new background to his phone.

When he comes back, the dildo is sitting in a warm water bath.

He orders you to lie back and you oblige immediately.

Turn to page 183.

Daddy pulls brings the heated dildo into bed and runs it across your nipples, drags it down to your pussy.

He spreads your lips with his fingers and inserts the dildo inside you.

Daddy moves the glass, pumping it in and out of you. Fucking you. Giving you pleasure, watching you writhe.

Without stopping the movement, he bends over and licks your clit drawing you to orgasm.

You go limp, knowing this is going to be a repeat performance.

Turn to page 186.

Daddy goes to cool it down in an ice bath. You apply some lipstick and take some sexy photos, set one as the new background to his phone.

When he comes back, the dildo is all frosty.

He orders you to lie back and you oblige immediately.

Turn to page 185.

Daddy runs the glass across your nipples, which perk up immediately.

He trails it down your stomach and spreads your lips with his fingers.

He spreads your lips with his fingers and inserts the dildo inside you.

Daddy moves the glass, pumping it in and out of you. Fucking you. Giving you pleasure, watching you writhe.

Without stopping the movement, he bends over and licks your clit drawing you to orgasm.

You go limp, knowing this is going to be a repeat performance.

Turn to page 186.

You could really use some extra support lately. You've realized that it takes courage to be vulnerable and are grateful to have someone who creates this safe space for you.

What area could you use extra support in?

You haven't been eating well and want some guidance with meals. *Turn to page 187.*

You want some extra words of affirmation to help with your confidence. *Turn to page 192.*

You need a check in every night on the phone when you aren't together. *Turn to page 195.*

You confide in Daddy that you want some guidance with nutrition. You've been struggling with snacking a lot lately…your guilty pleasure: chocolate chips straight from the bag. They are so good!

You don't want to go on a diet, but you do think you need a bit more structure in your life.

Daddy tells you to try adding some more vegetarian meals into your diet. *Turn to page 188.*

Daddy gives you a full-blown meal plan to follow so you don't even have to think about what you will eat. *Turn to page 189.*

Daddy says he could eat a little healthier too and you will do it together. *Turn to page 190.*

You raise your chin at him, you love burgers. A lot.
But you did ask for this…

You find some recipes for homemade veggie burgers
to try. You also decide to make a Japanese dish called
omourice, black bean taco wraps, and roasted veggie
grilled cheese.

Maybe it won't be so bad.

Turn to page 196.

This is what you need. Something really structured and easy to follow.

Overnight oats you can make ahead for breakfast. Bento boxes for lunch that help with portion control and are easy to switch up. Protein-packed dinners.

He did good…you will get a new list every Sunday with some new meals on it.

Turn to page 196.

"I've actually been wanting to eat a bit healthier too, baby," Daddy says.

You throw both arms around him. Everything is so much easier to stick to in a team.

You both write lists of what you like to eat and find that you actually enjoy a lot of the same foods.

Turn to page 191.

While you are prone to snacking, he doesn't drink enough water. This is something you are great at!

After lunch, you head to Target and get him a big water bottle with lines showing how many ounces he's had to drink so far in the day.

Daddy picks out a Bento box for you. It has different sections to keep options fun and full of variety for your lunches.

It will also make it feel like you are just snacking… your favorite!

Turn to page 196.

Sometimes it's nice to have some extra kind words sprinkled in throughout the day. Sure, you could look cute quotes up on the computer…but it's more meaningful when they come from someone you care for.

Daddy starts leaving post it notes on the bathroom mirror for you to see at random moments throughout the day.

Does Daddy compliment your physical features to boost your confidence? *Turn to page 193.*

Does Daddy notice and recognize all of the little things you do for him? *Turn to page 194.*

Daddy also texts you one thing he loves about your body every single day at noon—even if he's with you!

Today he texted you how much he loved how your breasts felt in his hands. They were the perfect size, almost like they were created just so he could hold them.

He better not get any weird ideas about writing romance novels because then he won't have as much time to play with you.

Turn to page 196.

He also texts you small praises every day at noon (how does he remember to do that?).

He compliments things you do and it makes your heart beat so quick you are worried it will run itself out of town.

Today he texted you how much he loves that you keep chocolates and Gatorade by the bed…just in case he needs quick replenishment during a session.

You do happen to be pretty thoughtful. Maybe you aren't the only lucky one around here…

Turn to page 196.

You've got a lot going on. Even if it's just a five minute chat to give a quick rundown of the day and say "goodnight, sleep well," you need to hear his voice.

"I'm sorry, baby. This fell through the cracks a bit lately," Daddy says.

"We are both responsible for our own needs," you say. "And I need you."

"You got it. I'm here."

Turn to page 196.

Things have been going so well in your d/s dynamic. Daddy asks if you want to move into his apartment and take your relationship to the next level.

You tell him you aren't ready for a romantic commitment yet but want to keep the d/s relationship going. *Turn to page 197.*

You tell him you are only interested in d/s. That's all you'll ever be. *Turn to page 198.*

You thought he would never ask! When is too soon to move in? *Turn to page 199.*

It takes you a while to warm up to new relationships. For now, you are enjoying getting to know him. There's no rush on your end.

You do offer to have standing committed sleepovers every Friday night. It will be a standing date you can both look forward to.

Daddy offers you a small drawer for your pajamas and toothbrush.

You decide to accept. For now.

The end.

You signed this contract only for the d/s experience. You aren't looking for anything additional.

Daddy says he understands and will keep the dynamic professional from now on.

The end.

You have really significant feelings growing for Daddy. You are so relieved to hear that they aren't one-sided!

"When are you going to help me move in all my things?" You ask.

"Immediately…after I'm done with this." Daddy takes you to the bedroom and ties you down for a welcome home session.

The end.

Acknowledgements

Daddy, thank you for keeping every single day an adventure. I promise to continue earning your love and trust, and never take you for granted. And for this book being published I would like a unicorn. Please.

Ravven, you are a force that blooms in nighttime while the rest of the world sleeps. Thank you for envisioning and creating a space for us to all choose our own adventure.

My fellow Corvids—it is a privilege to be surrounded by such genuine talent and generosity. I'll always be in your corner.

Kayla, I know you will walk the best path for you. No path is perfect but feeling at peace with yourself is the real treasure. I'm so proud of you for all you've accomplished.

Aimee Nicole is a chronically ill/disabled, queer poet currently residing in Rhode Island. She holds a BFA in Creative Writing from Roger Williams University and has been published by various lit mags. For fun, she enjoys overusing her public library system and has recently discovered the art of nail charms. Her collections include Daily Worship published by Laughing Ronin Press and Panoramic published by Curious Corvid Publishing. You can find her on Instagram @aimeenicole525 posting terrible selfies and pictures of her oversized cat.